HER MANE ESCORT

J.A. BELFIELD

HER MANE ESCORT

Published by J.A. Belfield
www.jabelfield.com

Copyright © 2018 Julie Anne Belfield

Previous published 2012 as Escort to Insanity in the Make Believe anthology

All rights reserved. No part of this publication may be reproduced, distributed, or transmitted in any form or by any means, including photocopying, recording, or other electronic or mechanical methods, without the prior written permission of the publisher, except in the case of brief quotations embodied in critical reviews and other non-commercial uses permitted by copyright law.
This book is a work of fiction. Names, characters, places, and incidents are either the products of the author's imagination or are used fictitiously. Any resemblance to actual persons, living or dead, businesses, events, locations, or any other element is entirely coincidental.

Cover art by J.A. Belfield.
10 9 8 7 6 5 4 3 2 1

ALSO BY J.A. BELFIELD

BEGINNINGS
THE WOLF WITHIN
BLUE MOON
CAGED
HEREDITARY
UNNATURAL
ENTICED
CORNERED
THE THERAPIST

NOTE FROM THE AUTHOR

First of all, thank you for picking up this copy of *Her Mane Escort*.

Some of you might remember it as being titled *Escort To Insanity* from way back in 2012, when it was published by my then publisher in an anthology titled *Make Believe*, and enjoyed it enough that you've returned for a second helping.

Be still my heart.

And some of you will be reading this for the first time. For whom I have equal depths to which my warm and fuzzies are a-fluttering.

Initially, I'd hoped to republish this little story of mine back in January, but life stepped on my plans for this year and forced me to take a step back for some much needed me-time. But I didn't give up on the idea of re-sharing this one with the world, because I love Ben, I love Nicole. I love the possibilities of their story, should I ever choose to visit them again for a little more craziness.

Whoever I write, whatever I write, I love the idea that there could always be more for them, for it. More than the mere words I've trapped within pages. More that I could do *with* them, should I so wish.

I also love that this one leaves the reader's mind filled with possibilities of their own, their own fantasies of where Ben and

Cole could, or should, go from here. And you should share them with me, if you do. You should totally share them with me.

For now, I'll just shut up, and let you read on.

Enjoy.

J.A. Belfield x

For the readers, who keep me keeping on.

1

"Urgh." I marched the width of my living room for the hundredth time, before wedging my stilettos into the shag-pile in front of the mirror. "Why do I subject myself to such …" I threw up my hands.

My tenant's reflection stared back at me from over my shoulder. "Craptapular evenings just to keep your flipping family happy?" One brown eyebrow rose above the sardonic expression in Kellie's hazel eyes.

"Yes, but …" I groaned and leaned forward, teasing my ebony fringe into perfect alignment and prodding at my French twist. "I can't believe I let you talk me into this. I mean, an escort, for goodness sake." A quick appraisal assured my black cocktail dress hugged where it should beneath my scarlet swing coat. "Like I'm some bloody saddo incapable of acquiring a date of her own."

"You have nabbed a date. That's the whole point."

"Okay, incapable of nabbing a date that doesn't cost me five grand for a few hours of his time."

"Five grand? Holy frickin' cow, Cole."

I met her reflected gaze. "You gave me the bloody number."

"Yeah, because they had prices starting from fifty quid."

"Fifty quid was for a date with Quasimodo. No point doing

this if I'm not going to take something to keep the vultures off my back."

"True." She nodded. "Very true … but …" At the chime of the doorbell, she spun away, as I whirled on the spot. "Forget it," she said, already moving for the hallway. "I'll see for myself what five grand worth of man looks like."

Frozen in place, I could only listen as she vanished into the hallway and her socked feet brushed over the floorboards. The catch twisted. The front door whooshed open.

"Nicole Harrington?" Disbelief tinged the deep, masculine tone.

"Would you like me to be?"

As I thought of what confronted him, Kellie in her Snoopy fleece shorts, peeling and faded Iron Maiden T-shirt, and hiking socks that had long ago lost any elasticity, I snorted out a laugh.

"Ignore her," I said. "She's just my tramp of a housemate. Come on in."

"What'd you do that for?" Kellie said. "I almost had him."

A deep chuckle preceded the delicate clop of a shoe on the floorboards. A moment later, one black clad shoulder peeked around the living room door, followed by a shock of honey blond hair and amber eyes.

Nice.

His left eyebrow arched up. "Nicole?"

Head tilted in an attempt to see the rest of him around the door, I nodded. "My friends call me Cole. Might be best if you stick to that this evening."

He crossed the room in a few easy strides, his hand already outstretched. "Benjamin Gold." He smiled down at me as I slid my fingers across his. "And I very much doubt you want to know what my friends call me."

I breathed out a small laugh. "I'll be sure not to ask." Ignoring Kellie's mimes of approval behind the escort's back—ones that looked suspiciously like she groped an invisible butt with her face screwed up—I pointed toward the door. "Shall we?"

"Of course." He spun for the exit, sending a nod toward Kellie as she snapped to attention. "Nice meeting you."

"You, too." She smiled.

I trailed behind Benjamin as he led the way to the exit and opened the front door. My sole had barely hit the outer deck, when fingers clamped around my upper arm and hauled me back into the hallway.

"What the heck, Kel—"

"Listen," she hissed. "For freak's sake, don't sleep with him. Something that cute'll cost you a small mortgage to pay the extra fees."

"Please." I rolled my eyes. "I'm not you. The advice is unwarranted."

"Good point." She patted my arm and released me, but grabbed hold again as I went to step away. "On second thought, do it. Besides the fact that you can afford it, you need the action, babe."

I pried her fingers from my bicep. "Bye, Kellie."

"What? I'm right, though, aren't I? You need to get you som—"

"Goodnight, Kellie."

"Fine, fine. Have fun."

Beneath the first snowflakes of the season, I began my descent toward where my 'date' waited at the garden gate.

"Meanwhile, I'll stay here," Kellie continued. "Alone. Probably get accosted by a burglar and have to deal with him all on my own." Her sigh arrived heavy, before she added, "Not that I'll mind if he's hawt."

"With a bit of luck, he'll look like a troll and carry you off to his bridge," I said, pivoting to face her. "And then I'll find a housemate who actually pays their rent."

She stuck out her tongue at me as I spun to walk away.

A silver Mercedes hummed at the kerbside beyond the gate, a shadowed outline all I could see of the driver.

"I prefer my own vehicle to the more impersonal ones of the agency," Benjamin said. "Hope you don't mind."

Had it been a rust-bucket Allegro, or something else equally hideous, my answer would have been a resounding *no*. Instead, I shook my head, smiling when he opened the rear door with a wave of his arm.

Heat blasted from the vents within—a vast comparison to the chilled winter evening—and the interior smelled of freshly-treated leather when I settled into my seat.

Once Benjamin had closed my door, dark eyes met mine in the rear-view mirror. Though the driver didn't turn, I found myself grateful when the other door opened and Benjamin slid in beside me.

He tapped the back of the driver's seat. "Horton Gallery, Drake."

Without a word uttered, the car eased away from the kerb as smooth as a spectre. The soft drone of the engine seemed to lull us into passivity, while the delicate handling of the vehicle barely swayed me in my seat. Streetlamps spilled their glow through the windshield, though they barely penetrated the tinted glass of the rear windows.

"You needn't worry." At Benjamin's murmur, I angled my head to see him and found his eyes already aimed my way.

"Worry about what?"

"About what your friend said back at the house." His teeth glowed white with his smile. "I'd never dream of charging for sex I'd initiated."

Twenty minutes of evening-debriefing later, we stepped arm-in-arm through the entrance of Horton Gallery. Snow dusted the shoulders and hood of my scarlet coat and of Benjamin's black jacket, and an upward glance showed even more clinging to the tips of his hair like diamante ornaments.

I shrugged out of the damp garment, and like the gentleman I'd paid him to be, Benjamin took it from me. After a promise to ensure it would be hung somewhere to dry, he weaved his way toward the cloakroom, leaving me to stand alone in the high-ceilinged foyer.

Beyond the double doors ahead, people milled about, nodding and smiling, while their twitchy or glazed eyes exposed their boredom. Each and every one of them wore more in value than they'd donate when the charity auction began—if not in clothing, then most certainly in the adornments that battled with the overhead chandeliers for impressiveness.

No doubt my lack of jewellery would earn me a few stares.

"Ready?"

Benjamin's voice snapped me from my bitter appraisal, and I nodded, hooking my fingers over the crook of his offered arm. "Into the lion's den we go."

"Trust me," he said, leading the way, "this is *not* a lion's den."

I went to ask what he meant, but the second we stepped from the foyer, Angela Hopberry accosted us.

"*Dar*ling." Her puckered coral pink lips did their usual air kisses in the direction of my cheeks. "How lovely that you came." The moment she straightened, her attention roamed over Benjamin like a wave across the beach. "You're a dark one, Cole—keeping it quiet about the new trophy."

I released a sigh. "Benjamin, this is Angela. Angela, Benjamin."

Angela had yet to remove her gaze from my partner. "And you've been seeing Cole how long? What line of business are you in? You're not a local boy, are you?"

Benjamin didn't even bat an eye. His hand slid around my back, drawing me closer. "Coley snared me …"

I bristled. *Coley?*

"… four days, seven hours, and approximately twenty-three minutes ago …"

Christ, don't overdo it. Though, that *had* been about the time I'd booked him.

"… I have ties in the motoring industry, and no … I'm not from around here." He grinned. "You have seventeen left."

Angela's lips hovered in an 'o' of non Comprendre.

"It was a joke." When her expression didn't change, he added, "I thought maybe we were playing twenty questions?"

"Oh." Angela swatted at him, giving a tinkled laugh that didn't quite reach her still confused stare. "I see I shall have to keep my eye on you."

"You do that." He nodded with a smile. "And while it was lovely meeting you, I fear my young lady requires refreshment."

Before either Angela or I could protest, Benjamin's arm tightened across my back and led me away.

"That was a little rude," I said, once we were out of earshot.

"Yes, well ... I'm not here to keep Angela entertained. My job is to ensure you have a good night. And you'd begun to look as though you'd rather be somewhere else." Benjamin nabbed a flute of champagne from a passing silver tray and handed it to me, grabbing a second for himself. "Now, tell me, why have you come here tonight when you've been tense since the moment we stepped through the entrance?"

Because I have no choice. Because my father will probably disown me if I falter in my dance steps to his tune any more than I already have. "I thought being an escort meant you just nodded and smiled in all the right places ..." ... *while warding off letchy exes who can't accept I've moved on.*

He chuckled. "Sorry, Cole, but you should have booked one of the less refined options if you wanted a date without a brain."

"That's not what I meant," I said.

"I know. Just teasing." His arm slid tighter around my back, his fingers hooking over my far hip.

I ignored how good it felt to be held when I hadn't been in so long.

2

For almost an hour, I avoided detection by said 'letch' before he finally caught up with me. As I stared at one of the auction pieces, my head tipped to mirror Benjamin's beside me, the chill along my left side warned of Tony's arrival.

His chest brushed my arm, lips infringed on my personal space, and breath sweated my ear with his whispered, "Figured out what it is, Cole?"

Benjamin shifted in my periphery, and a step brought him to face me in a way that spoke volumes, especially with his left hand claiming my waist. "Can I help you?" he asked.

Tony's smirk faltered for a second, before his smarmy façade reclaimed his face. As though Benjamin hadn't even spoken, he turned to me. "I didn't realise you were bringing a guest, Cole. You should have said."

"I did …" Though I attempted to hold steady, my gaze averted from his as fast as it connected. "… to the name on the invitation for the R.S.V.P.'s."

His head immediately snapped up and round, eyes searching the room—probably looking for Belinda Watton, the event organiser, so he could let rip about being kept out of the loop.

From his dark, oily hair, his cool green eyes, to his lean body perpetually draped in the most impeccable fabrics, just the sight of

Tony Lawson set my teeth on edge, and I wondered how I'd ever stomached him for the six months I had. If not for my father's encouragement—*more like demands*—for me to make it work, I'd have dumped the slime-ball within the first hour. When he told me he intended to tame me and ensure I carried his offspring, because between the two of us we could create beautiful people to continue the Lawson Legacy, I should have dumped Champagne on his head.

Pity my calling off what he considered to be a written-in-stone engagement hadn't dampened his ideals. For the past three and a half years, the arse had continued to treat me like his personal property while following a whole different set of rules for himself.

"Is Jackson here?" Tony's gaze swung back to me, his mask once more in place, but his even tone couldn't disguise the intent of his words. He wanted to know if my father approved of another man escorting me to a social event. "I haven't seen him anywhere."

"He couldn't make it." Hence the reason I'd been forced to represent the all-important family name. "He sends his apologies, though."

"He should have mentioned if you had no one to bring you." His clammy hand touched my shoulder—until a nudge of my body by Benjamin broke the contact. "I could have saved you—"

"I don't need you to save me from anything, Tony." My teeth ground. "I've moved—"

"She's always a little tetchy at the beginning of the evening." Tony smiled in Benjamin's direction, thumbing toward the rear of the room. "Bar's that way. I always find a few Chardonnays help loosen her up. Be a pal and get some down her for me ..."

What sounded like a low growl rumbled from Benjamin.

"And as for you, Cole?" Tony's knuckle chucked my chin. "I'll come find you later."

As he sauntered off with his cloying air of self-importance, Benjamin glared after him, the muscles in his jaw rigid. "Who. The. hell. Was that?"

My nose wrinkled beneath my grimace. "My ex. Dumped for being a dick."

"With a capital D. Is he always like that?"

I gave a small nod. "Pretty much."

Benjamin set his honey eyes back toward me, and the tension provoked by Tony's presence seemed to fade from my shoulders. "No wonder you look as though you'd rather be anywhere but here."

I stared up at him, nerves dancing in my stomach. He stood close to me—even more so when he ducked his face toward mine, and his lips skimmed from my cheek to my ear.

"Stay close to me," he murmured. "I'll protect you."

For the following ninety minutes, I gave Benjamin the reins. Each time his arm stiffened around my back and steered me in a different direction, I didn't once question his decision. It wasn't as though the room held anyone I had a desire to speak to, anyway. Besides, the glimpses I caught of Tony each time gave more than enough reason for me to trust Benjamin's instincts.

Five further accosts, and a few Martini's later, Benjamin drew me to stand behind a glass sculpture that resembled a screwed-up wad of cling-film. "This place is beginning to drive me crazy."

Not half as much as it bothered me, I'd have wagered.

"My entire role balances on my ability to ensure a woman has as pleasurable an evening as possible."

My eyebrow arched up. *I'll bet.*

"Not like that." He ran a hand through his hair, blew out a breath. "I feel like I'm failing you." His frown made me believe a Benjamin failure had never happened before. "Listen, Cole. How much longer are you expected to show your face here?"

My father's orders from a week before clanged through my head: 'You *will* go to the charity auction, young lady. No argument. It's high time you accepted the family name and what that entails. And you *will* represent the family name for the entire evening. Do you understand me?'

I also recalled my meek response.

With a heavy sigh, I grimaced up at Benjamin. "Until it ends."

He growled—actually growled—at me.

"Tell me, Benjamin." I folded my arms. "Do you usually complain to your date about where she asks you to escort her?"

"No."

"Then—"

"But my date doesn't usually look as though she'd rather be prying out her own fingernails with pliers than socialising with a bunch of shallow-minded folk who haven't quite mastered the art of smiling with their eyes."

"They—"

"You're better than these people, Cole. Let me take you somewhere else. Somewhere I can prove to you that a night out with me can be enjoyable."

"I …" *can't*. I sighed as it dawned on me how much his offer appealed, even if the words had described my life to a T.

He continued to gaze down at me, expectancy and hope gleaming in his eyes, and I knew there and then he'd never understand my reasoning.

Rather than try to explain, I took my usual coward's route. "Excuse me. I have to go to the ladies' room."

Coral tiles, pine disinfectant, and a bouffant of ash-blonde hair greeted me as I pushed through the door into the toilets. The woman poked at high strands that resembled wire wool as she leaned over the counter, puckering her red lips at the mirror. She barely even offered a glance my way as I ducked past into the first cubicle.

I closed the door and leaned back against it. Beyond the barrier, footsteps clopped to the exit, telling me the bouffant bird left, and as a heavy sigh heaved my chest, my lids lowered.

What on earth had made me think an escort would simplify the evening? Why the heck had I listened to Kellie and her stupid idea? More than that, why couldn't the agency have sent a pretty boy who simply looked good on my arm and knew when to keep his opinions to himself?

For as long as I could remember, I'd never gone against my

father's wishes. Nothing had ever seemed solid enough to fight for. Though, the older I grew, the more independent I became, and the more breaking free dangled like bait waiting for me to snap it up in my jaws. I barely understood the hold he seemed to have—not just over me, but over Mother, too—so no way would a stranger comprehend my life.

I rolled my eyes at myself as they opened. Why did it even matter when I wouldn't see Benjamin once the night ended, anyway?

I doubted he'd agree to a second event with the Parade of Pretentiousness.

I checked my watch as I spun and hiked up my dress. Only nine-twenty—meaning I had at least two more hours before I could acceptably leave. *Urgh.*

The bathroom door swung with a suction-like pop, and heels clipped into the room. I tracked them to the sinks, only half-registering the second shove of the door.

"Lois, darling."

Lois Cambridge could have single-handedly kept Tiffany's in business with the bling she forever flashed. The speaker—Clara Edington—held little more appeal with her pandering to the wealthy in a bid to snare a rich husband.

I sent a silent prayer of thanks that I'd been enclosed prior to the entrance of those two.

"Did you see him?" Clara asked, her voice taking on a conspiratorial edge.

"See who?" Lois's voice dropped to an exaggerated whisper, as though joining in some kind of secret game.

"Your ex. I swear I saw him earlier with Cole."

Say what?

"My ... ex?" Either Lois hadn't recently split with anyone, or she'd split with so many she had trouble figuring out which one. "Sorry, who?"

My question exactly.

"That hunk of yours you brought to the Mardi Gras fiasco last month ..." An event *I* had managed to wiggle out of. "... You know, the one with the golden hair and muscles to die for?"

My entire body stiffened.

"What was his name again?"

Please don't say it, please don't say it ...

"Benjamin?" Utter shock dripped from the singular word. "Benjamin's here?"

Though Clara didn't verbally respond, I imagined her smug nod of satisfaction.

"Benjamin's here?" Lois asked again. Silence followed, then, "Oh, crap."

"Oh, darling. Bad breakup, was it?"

"Um ... not ... really." Lois couldn't have sounded more uncomfortable—and the realisation of what capacity she'd been with Benjamin that night sent a wash of horror through me. "Benjamin ... and I were ... barely together long enough for ... um ..."

"Pity. The guy's yummy. Darling, you *must* say hello." A clop of a heel followed—like poor Lois had been yanked forward. "And who knows ..." The bathroom door squeaked open. "... he might even be pleased to see you. Goodness knows, Cole's barely in his leag—" The door whooshed shut.

My lips popped open in the ensuing quiet, hanging there a split second. "Oh, Christ—Benjamin."

The bathroom stood empty when I flew from the cubicle, and I dived through the door, landing myself amongst the minglers of the toilet passage with less dignity than a spread-eagled turkey.

"Excuse me." I shuffled between two of my father's acquaintances while hoping like crazy they wouldn't stall me to talk.

I could imagine the scene if Lois reached Benjamin first, could picture the knowing glances she'd send me. She'd know I'd hired him. Worse than that, she'd know no obstacle stood in her way of flirting and would no doubt attempt to score for herself.

No way could I tolerate *that* for an entire evening. The socialite bongos would spread the gossip faster than a bushfire. *Cole's Date Stolen by Lois—Hear All About It!*

Please be where I left you.

Worst case scenario, I thought, as I peered over shoulders and dodged bodies on my way to the cellophane sculpture, if Lois and her cheerleader got to him first, I'd just stroll right on past and make a hasty exit alone.

I caught the flash of golden curls, right where I left them —him. *Yes*.

As though he sensed my approach, he turned, and as his gaze swung around until it connected with mine, his lips started to curve before quickly twisting into a frown.

Did I look that flipping harried?

"What's wrong?" he asked, the second I reached him.

Grabbing his arm, I yanked him to follow without breaking stride. "Time to go."

"What's he done?"

"Who?" My eyes scoured every inch of the room for possible ambush.

"That idiot ex of yours."

"What?" I glanced back at him, almost stumbling as I rounded a deserted chair. "Oh—not him. I'll explain. Let's just get outside first."

3

A blanket of white covered the pavement, but Benjamin's hands at my elbow and waist helped keep me upright. I explained the hasty escape, his steps lengthening with each revelation until we'd rounded the corner and stood out of sight of the building's entrance.

He tucked in a wayward hair poking from my hood and tickling my cheek. "I'm so sorry."

"Hazard of the job, I guess." A gust blew beneath my dress, freezing my bum cheeks and making me wish I'd worn tights instead of stockings, and a huge shiver wracked my shrug.

"You're freezing." He opened his jacket, unzipped his inner pocket, and retrieved his phone. "I'll call for the car."

After the asphyxiating atmosphere of the gallery, of the sheep flocked within there, the fresh night air hit my brain like a dizzying drug I couldn't quite get enough of, and I found myself reaching to stall him. "Not … yet."

"Okay." He smiled, slipping the mobile back in. "What did you want to do?"

I shrugged, my palm lifting along with the action. "I've no idea."

"Well, maybe we should at least walk. Keep your blood pumping … while we decide what to do."

"Not much *to* do." I took his offered arm and allowed him to tuck me in close to his side, following his lead when he stepped down off the kerb and into the road. "If I go back in there with you, they'll be waiting to pounce. If I go back in alone, they'll think I've been dumped mid-evening, and Tony'll turn into his usual drink-fuelled-paw-monster. If I don't go back at all, my father'll go absolutely nuts in the morning." I blew out a breath as we climbed the opposite kerb onto the pavement that ran the length of the local park. "No matter what I do, the evening's a mess."

"And it's my fault."

"That's not what I mea—"

"Maybe not. But it's still the truth." He ducked as though to shield me, as breeze-provoked flakes tumbled down from an overhanging branch. "How about you let me make it up to you?"

Foot hovering mid-step, I peered up at him.

He chuckled. "Not like that." His arm unhooked mine and slid around to my back, nudging me forward with gentle persuasion. "I meant, you should let me show you the kind of evening you could have had."

"You really like to earn your keep, don't you?"

"Yes, ma'am."

Tucking my hands into my coat pockets, I smiled.

For a handful of beats, we didn't speak, merely wandered our way along the footpath, snow crunching beneath our feet with each step. My mobile weighed heavy in the clutch-bag I had wedged beneath my right arm, and the temptation to call a taxi and slink home beckoned. The mere idea of joining Kellie in a PJ-and-chocolate fest, curled next to the radiator while watching a crappy horror, almost had me snatching the phone out … until reality kicked in— and with it the realisation that the second I got home, I'd have to hear all my father's voice messages on the answer phone. I'd never told him I had a mobile for good reason.

On top of that, I'd have to hear Kellie's tirade about my stupidity at turning down the chance for a half-decent night.

"Okay." My nod fuzzed my hair beneath my hood. "What did you have in mind?"

"Ever heard of Flunkies?"

I laughed. "I'd have to say not. What is it?"

"The. Best. Doughnut. Bar. Ever. And it's open all night." His face peered beneath my hood. "You game?"

"Hmm, let me think ... doughnuts ... how far?"

"Other side of here." He wrapped his fingers around the bars of the wrought iron gate to Mersion Park.

The entrance squawked a little beneath the nudge of his hand with no bolt or padlock to hold it secure. Beyond the poor barrier, patches of snow coated the ground. More shrouded the enclosing hedgerow that stood sentry alongside the fence and prettied the trees, turning what could have been downright creepy into a winter wonderland, as each crystallised droplet sparkled in the dotted lamplight.

I halted. "Why do we need to go through the park?"

He shrugged. "We could go around." He pointed off to the right, toward where the end of the street and the park perimeter faded to shadow, too far away for any kind of clear definition. "But the park's a shorter route. And the paths will be gritted." He turned back, his gaze travelling from my feet to my face. "I figured it the fastest route."

I drew in a deep breath, peering once more into the abandoned plot. Nothing within set any alarm bells a-ringing. Certainly, nothing about the man beside me did—and hadn't since the moment he'd collected me from home. "Okay," I found myself saying, "lead the way."

The quietness we left behind seemed like a riot ground next to that of the deserted park. Though snow lined the trees either side, small icy patches still clung to the path, and would have foiled my steps if not for the grip of my killer heels.

"You often go to parks after dark?" I asked.

"I don't really need to." His hold tightened on my arm when my foot slipped an inch. "There's a vast patch of woodland around a half mile from my home. I just go there when the mood dictates."

"In the dark?"

"Night-time's the best. Besides the added challenge of visibility, the entire aura of the space alters the moment the sun dips and the moon rises to take her place."

My eyebrows rose a little. *Deep.* "You must really love it there."

"Certainly do. Less people traffic means more wildlife, too."

"Surely that just makes it more dangerous?" I'd heard badgers could get pretty mean.

He shrugged. "Had a family of Kite move in for the winter. I think they must have got confused and missed the mark on their real destination."

"Senile birds." My fingers wiggled in mock horror. "Terrifying creatures. That the best you got?"

"No. There's also a fox and his family, an entire army of scary rabbits ... lions ..."

"Lions? In Hereford?" A small laugh escaped.

"You'd be amazed by what you see when you wander around at night, Cole." Although his lips curved up, and only humour dominated his tone, his eyes held a seriousness I struggled to interpret—one that sent a shiver through me and not from the cold.

"In the woods, I mean," he said with a low chuckle.

Of course he did. I pulled my coat tighter around my neck.

"Dare to find out?" His low voice seemed to hold a bunker-full of promises as he gestured toward the infestation of trees that passed as the park's woodland.

If you go down to the woods today ... As the childhood nursery rhyme spun through my mind, my body stiffened.

"Relax, Cole." A chuckle. "I'm just kidding." He released my elbow, his arm sliding around my back.

For some reason, the flippant humour in his tone, the security of his hold, seemed to ease the tension claiming my shoulders. While the lack of sound in the park should have unnerved, it didn't, and my heels once more picked up their lazy cadence.

"It's so quiet," I murmured, almost coming to a stop before Benjamin's arm nudged me forward. Even the drone of engines from roads I knew to be no more than a half mile away barely reached us.

"It reminds me of winter in the woods," he said. "Where nothing else exists beyond the perimeter your soul creates."

My gaze lifted toward him, though I saw only the red of my hood. "Sounds ominous."

He chuckled, low and throaty, drawing tightness to my stomach. "It was meant to sound enticing."

"Those doughnuts had better be pretty special," I muttered, ignoring the implication of his words—as well as the effect he seemed to be having on my body. "My toes are bloody freezing."

"I'll warm them when we get there." His gentle squeeze swayed me a little. A wayward branch trembled as he flicked it from our trail. "And I can vouch for the cruller ... though it's nowhere near as special as the company I'm keeping."

A slow smile spread my lips before I could stop it—until I remembered who I was with and our circumstances. "I'll bet you say that to all your dates."

"Actually—" His arm stiffened across my back, his fingers digging into my waist and bringing me to a halt.

I reached up for my hood, went to tug it back to see what had stumbled his flow, but barely moved it more than an inch when a guy, then a second and third stepped into our path.

Left to right, all three of them looked big enough to bruise a sumo, and pissed enough to throw a punch.

A gulp lodged in my throat.

"Benjamin Gold."

He knows them?

The one in the middle, who'd spoken, had hair the colour of fallen sycamore leaves and wore head-to-toe black like he was auditioning for a role as the *Milk Tray Man*. "What brings you to Horton tonight?"

"Just passing through, Ivan," Benjamin said. "Permit me to escort the lady elsewhere, and I'll gladly come back and discuss this with you."

"You and I both know it should have been 'discussed'"—he actually did air quotes—"prior to you being here. Little late for an appeal, wouldn't you agree?"

"I'd have to say not."

I really wanted to ask Benjamin what the heck he was supposed to be appealing for, but something told me not to take my attention off the men—especially the duo at Ivan's sides—who stood in attire no more flamboyant than the one they flanked. The only item missing from their secret service getup was an earpiece with coiled wire tucked into their jackets.

Ivan's attention skipped to me, like he'd only just noticed I stood there. "Maybe the lady could appeal to us on your behalf." The way his gaze trailed south gave me the creeps.

"The lady has nothing to do with this." Benjamin's voice held a deepness that bordered on gruff.

A low thrum of power seemed to surround us until my fingertips tingled, and my lips turned more numb. Without even a full understanding of the situation, my heart stumbled.

Benjamin's arm swung me against his chest, and his gaze dipped to meet mine.

Before my mouth could even open to ask, *What the bloody hell's going on?* Benjamin's hands gripped my waist, and he threw me so fast my eyes could scarcely decode the blurred outlines that whizzed past.

My bum met with something hard that vibrated beneath the blow.

My skull collided with something solid enough to send sparks sizzling through my brain.

Once they fizzled out, a heavy blackness moved in and coated my thoughts with the intensity of asphyxiation—until, like fireworks exploding beyond my visual shutters, light penetrated my lids with enough power to send an ache right through to the back of my eyeballs, jolting me from whatever shadows I'd retreated to.

I let out a sharp cry, jerked to the right, my head banging against something solid and as rough as old bark. With a groan, I pressed a hand to my head, finding tenderness beneath a duet of abrasions. As the harsh glare dimmed away, an inhuman growl rumbled through the trees until every hair erected along the curve of my spine.

When a hissing erupted like the woods had been struck by a sudden snake invasion, my eyes flicked open.

I let out a gasp, my mouth stretching into a ridiculous *O*, and snatched my legs up until my knees hit my chin.

The broad limb of a tree supported my rear around eight feet from the ground, and beneath my dangling feet, the craziest scene I had ever witnessed filled the air with growls and hisses and crashes and snaps, as rabid-looking beasts rolled about and attacked one another.

Against my better judgment, I stared harder through the melee, identifying what looked like a lion—*a freaking lion*—two panthers, and a black … *Pitbull?*

The side to side whipping of my head could scarcely keep up with the frantic darts, leaps, pivots, and lunges.

Tearing my gaze from the insanity, I made a rapid scan through the trees and foliage, wondering where the hell my date had gone and why the heck he'd … *Why the heck did he leave me here?*

No golden hair caught the moonlight, though. No broad shoulders clothed in black.

Way to go, Cole. You picked a date that dumps a girl in a zoo fed on rage.

I gave another rapid scan. Maybe I hoped a solution to my problem of being stuck in a tree above rampant beasties would suddenly appear. Maybe it would have—if my gaze hadn't landed on the scattered and shredded remains of clothing.

The kick-off of one of the panthers sent a strip of white fabric spiralling upward to meet me. As though on autopilot, my hand shot out to snatch hold of it and brought the scrap to my nose.

The cotton carried a muskiness blended with sandalwood that I hadn't realised, until that moment, I'd smelled the entire night.

Benjamin.

I let out a sob and searched the ground again.

No Benjamin.

Bastards had eaten him.

What if I'm their next meal?

As I studied the ground and realised only clothing remained of Benjamin, another sob erupted.

The lion landed from a dive. Its head turned my way.

When the feline's gaze connected with mine, I slammed a hand over my mouth. Like that could stem the sudden onset of hyperventilation.

The twin amber orbs somehow radiated concern and regret in a single glance, the spilling emotions making them appear far too human.

Benjamin.

I had no idea why his name popped into my head, but in the next half second, I studied the golden fur framing the eyes, the likeness to a certain someone *much* closer than I had any intention of accepting.

Insane.

The connection snapped as one of the panthers smacked into the lion's shoulder with a victorious roar and sent the lion soaring.

Shaking my head clear, I grabbed hold of a neighbouring branch and wriggled until my bum slid off its perch.

A small squeak escaped when my body dropped way faster than anticipated, followed by a cry I forced quiet when my shoulders burned against the strain, and my useless fingers slipped. As my feet hit the ground, my knees crumbled, the collision between my shoulder and the trunk saving me from a full-out tumble. I glanced toward the scrapping animals.

The lion could barely be seen amongst the attack of black beasts —until the golden head thrust upward, parting the way with the force of a volcano. Its teeth locked around the throat of the Pitbull, and with a toss of its powerful head, the lion sent the dog flying until it bounced off a tree with a piercing yelp.

In the next breath, roars, hisses, and growls set my pulse rocketing, as the two panthers attempted reciprocation, and the three felines blurred in a dizzying roll—away from me.

Move yourself, Cole. Snapping my attention from the tussling cats, I took off in the opposite direction as fast as my stupid heels would allow.

By only the faint glow of the winter moon, I speed-trotted around trees and branches, getting sprayed by a fine mist of snow any time I didn't veer wide enough. More than once I cursed my blasted footwear as my feet wobbled, my ankles almost twisting beneath the force of my unhinged steps. If not for the straps securing the shoes, I'd have kicked the offending articles off.

Come on, come on.

Around one trunk, and another, my breaths panted from me, each one seemingly shorter than the last.

A badly-judged dodge resulted in a scratch across my cheek, before the assaulting twig caught in my hair and yanked strands from their binding. I gave a low cry, tears threatening to well at the ridiculously terrifying situation I'd gotten myself into. I only prayed my feet carried me in the right direction.

Though, with the preceding luck of the night as a pointer, I'd probably end up travelling full circle and land myself right back into the thick of it all.

A quiet boom-boom pattern of noise chased me.

My chin whipped up and round, my eyes flittering in an attempt to see all directions at once.

Only branches waved like hag's fingers beckoning me closer.

The beat hit ground somewhere off to my right.

My head spun that way.

Shadows danced as wood and brush trembled in the breeze.

Tearing my gaze back ahead, I willed myself faster, arms winging back and forth with each manic step.

Something thumped right behind me.

I shrieked.

A heavy force rammed against my back.

The ground surged to meet my body, but a belt made of steel wrapped around my torso, pinning my arms before they could flail.

When my feet left the ground, and my body bulleted forward, breath evaded me. My mind caught up with the rapid haze of passing trees and the realisation that someone had grabbed me.

I opened my mouth wide, releasing a scream of banshee proportions, and kicked back like a mule.

A grunt told me I'd struck well—just as a hand slapped over my mouth. "Hush, they'll hear us."

Benjamin? Though the question actually left my throat as *'Em-um-im?'*

"Yes, relax." His panted breaths heated the side of my neck. "Dammit, Cole. Why couldn't you just stay put?"

Light headedness speared through my brain as the girder about my ribcage tightened with each bounding jolt of his body. Trees rushed toward us, Benjamin's weaving missing them by inches. Tiny screams squeaked from me at every turn.

The trees thinned and railings appeared through breaks in brush. I wanted to gush out a sigh of relief, except Benjamin's palm stalled even that.

"Get the gate," he said, aiming us straight for it.

My hand went to lift. His arms didn't allow it.

"The *gate*, Cole."

Hauling my knees up, I booted out with both legs the second we reached it, a clang ringing through the air as it shot outward to allow access.

Without breaking stride, Benjamin burst out onto the pavement, raced across the road to the opposite side of the street, and bolted into an alley as dark as a cavern.

My heels scraped concrete, my knees wobbling as my weight settled onto them.

The hand left my mouth, and Benjamin spun me until my back hit the side of whatever building hid us.

I gasped in a few breaths. "What the flipping heck's going on?"

He placed a finger to his lips.

"Do you know those men, Benjamin?"

With a little shush sound, his gaze left mine, and he stepped to the left.

My attention followed him into the faint spray of lamplight.

All of him.

All six and a half naked feet of him.

My eyes widened.

He reached out, wrapping his fingers around the corner of the wall. The movement sent a ripple through muscles across his chest, over a ridge-packed stomach, and all the way down to ... *Holy crap, that's big.*

"You have no bloody clothes on!" '*Cause they're shredded*, my mind hissed. Shaking my head, I forced my gaze north. "What the heck happened to you? Where the hell did you go?"

He pressed his finger back to his lips, still focusing somewhere out in the street.

"I can't believe you stuck me in a tree ..."

"Hush, will you?"

"… A tree! You bloody left me there. With those … those—"

His mouth smothered mine, and I gasped, hadn't even seen it coming. His tongue darted out; my low moan escaped. "Jesus, you taste good," he murmured. "But we need to get you out of here. Where's your mobile?"

"My …" As he stepped away, I peered down at my hands as though confused over their emptiness. "I lost my bag."

We both turned toward the park.

"Tell me you didn't lose it in there."

"I lost it in there."

He cursed, turned back to me. "Listen to me. You're going to take off your shoes—"

"What? It's sno—"

His palm cut me off. "You've already proved they slow you down. And I need you to run as fast as you can to the river car park. Drake will be there. Get in the car with him. Tell him where I am."

I nudged his hand down. "And you?"

He dropped to his knees, his fingers unleashing my shoes like he'd had a lot of practice. Once he'd slipped them off, he straightened and handed them to me. "I'm going for your purse."

"But—"

"Run."

"But—"

He darted back out into the street, his totally hot arse bouncing around beneath the lamplight, and left me standing in a dark alley in Horton with my feet fast going numb.

My body turned to go the way he'd ordered, but my head tried to send me back the other way. Car. Ben. Car. Ben.

A snarl ripped through the air.

I squeaked and bolted.

The end of the alley couldn't come fast enough. My stocking-clad feet trampled over stones and rubbish and who knew what else, each little stab accompanied by my string of inventive 'Ouch's. Breaths panted from me by the time I burst from the shadows onto the soggy mush of the street and angled left. Dashing along, I hoped nobody noticed the crazy, hyperventilating, vagrant-looking woman racing along as though pursued by the hounds of hell.

Thirty metres ahead, the orange glow of the car park lights lent a blush to the sparkling ground, where they peeked through the trees that separated the road from the river.

A minute later, I spotted the Mercedes.

Oh, thank God!

On feet frozen beyond feeling, I raced through the entrance. Straight to the car. Banged on the window.

Nothing.

I ducked forward, peering through the windscreen.

Empty.

I gave a small whimper.

A moment later, frustration fuelled temper, and I kicked the door, slapping the window. "Where the bloody he—"

Hands grabbed my waist.

I swung around. Raised my heels. Swung them down on my attacker.

"Bollocks!"

I flipped my arm up again and drove it back down.

A hand snaked round my wrist. "Quit! I'm not gonna hurt you."

My breath wheezed out, and I blinked the terror from my vision.

"Where's Ben?" Drake's gaze scanned me. His nostrils flared. "Oh, shit!" His hand released me. In the next second, the alarm bleeped, the lights flashing through the shadows. "Get in the passenger seat."

I didn't need telling twice. My bum met with leather as the engine sprang to life, and I snapped my seatbelt on.

"Where?"

"Mersion Park." I still panted a little. "This side. Benjamin was taking me for a cruller."

The car screeched through the gates. "Flunkies?" Despite his tense arms flipping the wheel to the right, Drake made the question sound like casual chat.

"Yes."

"Best doughnuts around. Idiot."

"Excuse me?"

"Not you." He twisted the wheel left, squeezing us between double parked cars with barely an inch to spare. "Benjamin. Risking it for bloody crullers."

"Risking what exactly?" I asked, gripping the door as the car swerved around a left corner and the park railings came into view.

"What?" He glanced my way, back to the road. "Oh, er … bumping into Ivan."

I frowned. "How do you kno—"

The car skidded over the sludge-covered road, grinding to a halt outside the gate Benjamin had charged us through.

Drake twisted to me. "Stay in the car."

Before I could respond, he exited the Mercedes and vanished into the park before his door had even slammed shut. I unclipped my belt and dived across to peer through the driver's window, eyes squinted like that would help me see beyond the hedge.

One minute passed. I massaged my toes in an attempt to circulate the blood.

Two minutes passed.

Three.

Jesus, where are they?

I flopped back into my seat and flipped the door catch. Chill air rushed through the gap as I swung the door open. Wetness sifted through what was left of my stockings as I stepped into the road.

"What part of stay in the car didn't you understand?"

My head snapped up to see Drake rounding the gate. I held my breath, releasing it slowly when Benjamin marched out behind him and straight to me.

His arms scooped beneath my legs and around my shoulders, and he deposited me back in the passenger seat. "Do you ever do as you're told?"

"Yes, often." As I met his gaze, his eyes turned a warm shade of honey and seemed to glow in the dimness. I swallowed. "Did you find my purse?"

He withdrew from the car without answering and shut me in.

The rear and driver's doors opened, and the both of them joined me. Without a word from either of them, the engine turned over, first gear was engaged, and Drake slid the car away from the kerbside.

I straightened in my seat after Drake had taken two left turns, heading us back toward river car park and away from my house. "You took a wrong turn."

He didn't answer, just stared straight ahead, both hands on the wheel.

I pointed behind us. "My house is that way." My panic might not have hit me full mode, but my voice still wavered and arrived a little shrill. "Where are we going? Surely, we're still not going to bloody Flunkies after this?"

"We're going somewhere safe," Benjamin said behind me.

I twisted to bring him into view. "My house is safe."

"Not any more it isn't."

"Wh …" I frowned, forced down a gulp. "What do you mean?"

"I couldn't find your purse, Cole. It wasn't there. If it was, I'd have sme—" He averted his gaze, drawing in a deep sigh. "I'd have found it."

"So … I'll change my locks."

He shook his head. "It's not that simple. The fact it was missing means that they most likely have it. Which means they may now have your address. As well as your keys. So—"

"Oh, my God! Kellie!"

"Who's Kellie?" Drake said, just as Benjamin's uttered, "Shit!" burst out.

"You have to take me back." I grabbed Drake's arm, my gaze on Benjamin. "We have to go back there."

"Cole, calm down." Benjamin reached over and pried my fingers from jerking Drake side-to-side. "Drake, where's your phone?"

With a bit of hip thrusting and prying, he retrieved it from his pocket, and Benjamin took it and passed it to me. "Call home."

Though my hands shook a little, I managed to enter the house number before pressing dial and sticking the phone to my ear.

Silence preceded static and the chirp of the ringtone.

I held my breath, mentally counting through the bleeps like a chant: *un-uhn, un-uhn, un-uhn* ... After the eighth round, the click of the answer phone sounded.

I hung up, dialled again, ignoring the weight of Benjamin's attention and distracted from the fact Drake still drove the wrong way at death-miles-per-hour.

Same amount of bleeps, same click, followed by, 'Hey, this is Cole and Kellie—'

I hung up. "No answer."

"She have a mobile?" Drake asked.

"Yes, but ..." I stared down at the phone, jaw tight. "I've never had to dial it. It's been stored in my mobile so long, I'm not even sure of the number. I mean, is it oh-seven-nine-eight, or oh-seven-eight-nine, or—dammit, I don't know."

"Try them both," Benjamin said. "We'll reach my place in a minute, anyway, and then I'll go check on her." His hand slipped through the seats, his thumb brushing across my cheek. "It'll be okay, Cole. I promise."

Taking a deep breath, I nodded. "Oh-seven ... oh-seven ..." I mumbled the combination of numbers beneath my breath, closing my eyes in concentration as I worked through the sequence like a long-forgotten song. *Just try the damn number*, I yelled at myself and began pressing buttons.

As the ring tone buzzed at my ear, the car made a sharp veer onto a road that put its suspension to the test. I sat up straighter, hand braced against the window as I peered into total blackness.

My pulse notched up a gear. "Where on earth are you tak—?"

I jolted at the connecting click through the phone line.

Static silence.

I looked across at Drake, his glinting eyes telling me he stared my way through the dark interior. "Hello?"

"Who's this?" Gruff didn't quite cover the answering tone.

"Oh, um ... I ... was after my friend. I think I may have the wrong number. So sorry to bother you."

"Whatever." *Click*.

"Charming," I muttered as the car quit its bouncing act and

rolled over a new surface that didn't threaten to wreck my teeth. A check through the windscreen showed glowing squares more commonly known as illuminated windows and a couple of parked vehicles. "Where—"

"My house." Benjamin climbed from the car, and a few seconds later, he opened my door. Before I could even swing a leg out, he reached in and hugged me against his chest.

Though my mind rebelled at the dominant gesture, I kept mute, instead calling home again. While Benjamin marched us across a rough lain drive, I checked out my surroundings.

What I'd have described as a wooden shack, had it not been two storeys high with a double frontage and a canopied deck that seemed to circle the building, loomed over us. The light I'd seen spilled from downstairs windows, while the upstairs ones stared back like a couple of unseeing eyes.

My gaze darted side-to-side, searching for neighbours.

Like something out of a post-apocalyptic movie, only deserted, snow-blanketed land spanned left and right, barely a tree or bush rising out of the darkness. The chirping tone at my ear at least lent an illusionary connection to normalcy.

Click. 'Hey, this is Cole and Kellie. Sorry we're not able to take your call at the moment, but if you leave a name and number, we'll do our best to get back to you,' we both sang, before Kellie's tag of, 'Or not!' ended the message. *Beep*.

"Kellie, if you're there, for goodness sake call me ... on ... how the heck's she going to call me?" When I glanced up at Benjamin, he rattled off a landline number, which I recited into the phone. "If you're asleep and ignoring the bloody phone, I swear to God, Kellie, I'll make you cook every night this week. Are you even listening to me?"

As I hung up on a sigh, Drake opened a door to the rear of the property, and we entered to a lit kitchen decked out with the same distressed appearance as the outside.

A chair scraped back from a generous table set to one side. The giant that evacuated it stared our way from beneath hair as ginger as a brandy snap, his wide eyes flitting left, right, left, right. He finally settled on a spot just above my shoulder. "Ben …" He said the word slowly. "What's going on?"

"Complications to the evening." Benjamin carried me straight to one of the counters and set me down with legs dangling.

"Understatement," Drake said. "Ivan Koposky is what really happened."

"Shit!" The redhead raked his fingers through his hair. "You think they were gunning for you?"

"No, just coincidence and …" Benjamin's gaze settled on me before fluttering away. "… distractions."

"You still owe him a shedload of dough from your last trespass, Ben. I thought tonight was supposed to be a straight in and out and no loiter? What the hell were you thinking?"

Beneath my frown, my attention flitted from male to male.

"Trying to Flunky-impress the female," Drake muttered.

Benjamin sent them a glare and turned back to me. As he caught one of my feet up, he frowned before his fingers pressed my cheek near the scratch I'd forgotten about. "You're hurt."

"And you're still naked. Do you often run around Horton with no clothes on, Benjamin?"

"No."

"Why were you …" A gulp started to wedge in my throat again as alternating flashes whipped through my mind: *scrapped clothes-lion-scrapped clothes-lion-scrapped*—I blinked. "Why were your clothes torn to shreds?" My gaze skimmed over him—fast, so I didn't have time to linger on any one solid, muscular spot. "And there're no marks on you—how is that possible?"

His golden eyes gazed into me, ensuring my throat obstruction expanded by at least fifty percent. After a few seconds, he pushed away and stalked from the room.

I stared after him before turning to the gingernut, who studied me like an alien had come for afternoon tea, and to Drake, who gave a small headshake, one corner of his mouth curved up in the barest of smiles.

Benjamin reappeared in the kitchen doorway, a pair of boxers in his hand. "How about if I just leave you to come to terms with what I suspect you've already figured out?"

Um ... huh? My mouth opened.

"In the meantime ..." He pointed at my hand and Drake's mobile I still hogged. "Keep trying your friend's phone."

The following minutes seemed to pass in a manic blur. While I tried differing combinations of the digits stuck in my head, Benjamin dressed and tossed orders at Drake and the redhead.

Mid-dial, for the seventh time, a fourth guy entered the fray, his attention falling on me like a hydraulic hammer. "Has anyone else noticed there's a cute feme sitting on the kitchen counter?" The Attila-the-Hun lookalike stoppered my throat for a moment as the darkest eyes I'd ever seen seemed to appraise me from head to toe. All while the loomer wore a leer on his chops. "So, who brought the entertainment, then?" he asked, when Benjamin shoved past him from the hallway.

"She's off limits. Cole meet Corey. Don't worry," he said, like he'd caught my momentary panic, "he's not as thuggish as he looks."

I went back to my task of trying new sets of digits, half listening to Benjamin re-cover the issue and his big plan for them to head off to Ivan's boss's condo and snatch back Kellie with whatever force they deemed necessary. All while I sat alone, in a strange house, in the middle of nowhere, worrying myself sick.

The dial tone at my ear stalled; the quiet connective click sounded.

"Hello," purred a smooth, deep voice.

My sigh arrived heavy. "Sorry, I think I must have the wrong number." *Again.*

"Tell me who you're looking for, and I'll be the judge of that."

For some reason, the hairs prickled along my nape. "My friend, Kellie."

"Cole, I presume? Why don't you put one of the Toms I can hear in the background on the line?"

Toms?

My heart stuttered as I glanced toward where the four men mumbled about infiltration and backup. No mention of heading to my house to check on Kellie. Did they already know she wouldn't be there? What hadn't Benjamin told me, exactly?

As though he'd sensed my scrutiny, his honeyed gaze spun to me. "Cole?"

The three other men quit talking and turned toward me, too, and my hand holding the phone reached out like it belonged to someone else.

Benjamin stepped forward. "Yes?"

I knew when the guy on the line began speaking because Benjamin's jaw set rigid, the muscles clenched in his cheeks, and a deep V cut a groove between his eyebrows.

"Twenty-five?" Anger laced the words as his hand fisted around the mobile. More quiet minutes passed, a flat expressionless glaze entering Benjamin's eyes, making him appear more terrifying than if he'd bared his teeth and screamed out the frustration pumping from him like a pulsed energy. Finally, he said, "Unharmed, or no deal."

He hit the disconnect button and faced the ceiling, his chest rising and falling like he struggled to contain himself.

"Twenty-five?" Corey asked.

Eyes still aimed heavenward, Benjamin nodded.

"But you only owe him two from the last time."

"Yep," Benjamin muttered.

"How's he justify—"

"Interest."

"But … we don't have twenty-five," Drake said. "We don't even have the two … do we?"

"Nope." On an extra deep inhale and exhale, Benjamin lowered his face and stepped back to me. "Keep this." He handed me the phone, his other hand brushing across my cheek. "I'll call you as soon as we have your friend." He gazed into me for seconds, seemed to want to say more, but turned away and nodded to the others. "Let's go get her."

From my perch on the worktop, I watched as the four of them trailed from the room like they were heading for nothing more pressing than a grocery-shopping trip.

Like they tackled potential kidnaps every day.

Because I was certain that was what had happened to Kellie. *Because of me.* The realisation turned my blood cold.

The second the front door closed on the departing men, leaving me surrounded by a strange house, totally unknowing of my location and one-hundred percent alone, my body began to tremble. I couldn't seem to stop it—just as I couldn't seem to halt thoughts of the evening rampaging through my mind. From the moment it truly sank in that I'd rather book an escort than tell my father where to stick his blasted orders, right up until the phone call that confirmed the only person in the world I considered a true friend had been dragged into danger.

And I'm just sitting here, I thought as I blotted away a rogue tear with my sleeve.

What else could I do? It wasn't like I could join Benjamin in whatever method he intended applying to get Kellie back—because the glint in his eye told me it didn't involve negotiations.

I didn't even know where they'd headed, anyway. Maybe I should have gotten at least that much info from the man before I'd handed the phone over to Benjamin.

Stilling, I stared down at the mobile in my hand. *Get it now, Cole.*

Dare I, though? Benjamin evidently wanted me out of the way while the men dealt with the situation.

All while Kellie was being held by ... *what?*

My mind whirled again, whizzing back to what I'd seen in the park. Back to that lion with eyes like ... like ... *Say it, Cole.*

"Eyes like Benjamin's," I whispered.

What did that say about the panthers?

"The panthers have Kellie."

Hand trembling, I hit redial as though on autopilot.

Only one ring buzzed through before the connection clicked.

"Yes?" The same smooth voice as before.

I placed the phone to my ear. "It ... it's Cole."

No response.

Tamping down my nerves and drawing on my heritage I tried so hard to ignore, I pushed forth. "I need to confirm the amount payable and the place of exchange for my friend."

A chuckle, then, "Does Benjamin know of this call?"

"That's irrelevant." I allowed a hint of the steel learned from my father into my tone. "Would you like your payment, or not?"

Another chuckle travelled the line. "Twenty-five. Beech Farm, on the main A-road out of Horton toward Leominster."

"Twenty-five pounds?"

"No."

"Twenty-five hundred?"

He sighed. "No, Ms Harrington. Twenty five K. I'll be seeing you shortly."

The line went dead.

Jesus Christ. Who were these people that they thought they could charge such ridiculous amounts just for a stroll in the bloody park? Some kind of crime organisation?

I glanced at the clock on the wall. Benjamin had been gone only ten minutes. The A-road the man spoke of stretched from the far side of town, meaning Benjamin had to bypass my house to get there. Could I make it before him? Even with a detour to grab the funds?

Who the hell was I trying to kid? I hadn't even any wheels.

My mind flashed to the outside driveway and the vehicles I'd seen there. *Where there're vehicles, there are* ... "Keys. Find the keys."

I hopped from the worktop, the tile floor cold against my soles. After scanning the visible surfaces and checking drawers, I headed for a dresser on the far side of the table and struck gold when I pulled open a glass-fronted door. Two key-fobs sat in a ceramic bowl, one for a Ford, the other for a Toyota. Something made me opt for the latter, and before I could change my mind, I shot from the house.

4

Thankfully, the keys worked in a RAV4, it had fuel in its tank, and did a decent job tackling the snow still littering the streets.

At the kerbside outside my house, I yanked on the handbrake and jumped from the vehicle, hopping to the porch like I travelled over hot coals rather than an ice-carpet. My front door had been left ajar—no doubt as a message—and I pushed through without pausing, tossing my useless shoes into the hall corner on my way to the lounge.

The red light of the answer-machine blinked like crazy. I hit the play button, slipping out of my coat as the messages ran through.

'Cole, where did you go, baby?' *Tony*. The evening's interaction with him seemed a lifetime away.

I slammed a hand down on *delete*, moving back into the hallway to mount the stairs.

'Nicole, what the bloody hell are you playing at?'

I sighed, before blanking out my father's voice and slipping into the spare bedroom that held my wardrobe of clothes.

Mud decorated the hem of the black dress I wore. My stockings looked like a *Rocky Horror Picture Show* aftermath. Off they came, tossed into the corner, to be exchanged for my black Versace jeans and black Pierre Cardin V-neck sweater. Onto my feet, I tugged

Tigger socks I'd stolen from Kellie for their softness, and a pair of designer biker boots my father hated me wearing.

After re-securing my hair in a ponytail, I jogged back down the stairs to the living room, where my father's tirade still rolled through speakers like something robotic.

'... mother is very upset ...'

Probably from listening to you rant on half the night.

A small door, halfway along the first wall, led to the cupboard under the stairs. Inside was where I stored my personal safe, with a combination I changed on a weekly basis. My eyes scanned the piles of notes within—ones I'd worked hard to save, because Father had insisted I prove my responsibility every week for him to keep me in his will.

Without hesitation, I pulled out a sack, shook it open, and began the transfer of cash until only five bundles remained.

'... I expect better of you, Nicole ...' my father's voice continued, as I ducked from the cupboard. 'You're a Harring—'

With my coat snatched up on route, I slammed the hall door shut on his voice and raced out of the house.

Fresh snowflakes splattered against the windscreen, marring my ability to see, even with the wipers on full whack. I drove along the A-road toward Leominster, and with seven miles clocked, no sign of any farm convinced me I'd missed the place, until I spotted two brick pillars at a harsh bend ahead of me. I squinted through the raining white at the seven-foot-high structures that supported gates left wide open and acted as pedestals for a couple of gigantic stone cats.

Cats—typical. "Got to be it," I murmured, slowing the car to a halt alongside them to read the brass plaques: Beech Farm.

For some reason, reaching there didn't exactly quell the nerves shivering through my body. Reminding myself of my quest—Kellie—I stuck the gearstick into reverse, backed up enough to make the turn, and weaved the Toyota between the gateposts.

The driveway, clear of snow, looked like a river of grey for the

Toyota's headlights to follow. Twin mounds of bordering white disappeared into dense clusters of trees on either side, while around fifty metres ahead stood the biggest farmhouse I'd ever laid eyes on. Seven illuminated windows and a broad door graced the front, overlooking a circular fountain where the driveway came to an end.

At blurred movement bundling into the car's path, I pounded my foot on the brake, gripping the wheel as the tyres made a slight skid to the left, and stared at a rolling duo of huge cats scrabbling at each other.

More cats.

With my heart boom-a-boom-booming, I blinked.

Only the flick of a tail remained in the glow of my headlights, before even that vanished into the trees on the right.

Releasing a sharp blast of pent-up breath, I loosened my fists and navigated the vehicle once more in the direction of the house. Toward, I suspected, the guy from the phone.

No other cars dotted the fountain-adorned roundabout when I parked. For a few moments, I sat studying my quiet surroundings. Despite the gentle efforts of the trees to shake the snow from their branches, everything seemed still. Too still.

Creepy.

Shaking off my musings, I grabbed up the sack of cash from where I'd set it in the passenger foot-well and climbed out of the vehicle to the kind of misleading insulation only snow brings. Other than the muted crunch of my boots against the powder, little sound reached my ears—not even the expected rustles of nocturne life.

Which only seemed to make the grounds all the more creepy.

At a sudden screech off to the far right, my entire body jerked as an involuntary gasp burst from me, and I spun toward the sound. Nothing stood there as the source, no animals or beasties prowled from the between the timber, and it took a few seconds of me scouring to realise I stood gawping with a hand pressed to my chest.

"Get a grip," I whispered, rolling my shoulders as I tightened my hand around the sack of cash.

Slamming the car door and staring up at the house, I couldn't help but notice the way it seemed to have been downplayed from the mansion it truly was. With the quality of the carpentry cladding its façade, it made me wonder the why behind it—did the owner just not like blatant opulence? Or maybe they just didn't want others to be too aware of the depth of their wealth.

Whatever their reasons, their efforts seemed inadequate when paired with the house's size. Although, considering the social circles I'd been brought up in, the luxury properties I'd been prettied up to visit, the building shouldn't have seemed that big, at all. Heck, my parents' house—my family home—covered more square footage.

Yet, the building still gave me pause, before I gave a mental shake and ordered myself forth.

Four stone steps led up to the front door, on which a brass knocker hung from a lion's head mount. I lifted the ring, dropping it against the wood, and the clash echoed through the night like a chime of doom as the tremble of my knees betrayed my anxiety.

At a gentle vibration through my hip, I glanced down and, catching a glow through the dark denim, worked out Drake's mobile. 'Corey' flashed across the screen.

I twisted and peered behind, wondering if they'd already arrived, if they already hid somewhere—if it had been one of them I'd seen tumbling into the trees—but the twist of a catch drew my attention back to the door. I shoved the phone into my pocket just as it swung inward and light spilled over me.

Ivan from the park stood in the opening, that same smugness on his face. "You surprise me. I didn't think you'd come."

"Why wouldn't I?" I asked, praying for my tone not to wobble and give away just how scared I really was. "A deal was struck, after all. The Harrington's aren't known for backing out." Father would have probably been proud at last—unless, of course, he learned of the circumstances leading to the deal, and the fact I'd taken my savings to bail out my best friend … *who only needs bailing out at all because of me.*

Ivan stepped back and inclined his chin. "You'd better come in, then."

Just like the exterior, white dominated the hall, on the walls, ceiling, even the furniture that Ivan guided us past across a parquet floor. With barely a falter in his flow, he gestured me to follow and disappeared around a high archway.

The corner I rounded took me into a library impressively crowded on all sides by floor-to-ceiling shelves that had been packed tight with books. In a wing chair in the centre sat Kellie, still donned in her fleecy shorts and tatty T and socks.

Her head whipped up as soon as I stepped into the room. A hoard of emotion spilled from her wide eyes, mingling with unspoken fear, determination, and pleading—definitely pleading.

After checking her over, surprised, yet relieved, to find no bindings on her, nor any marks, I sent her a small nod and gave my attention to the man at her side.

Not as tall as Ivan, but somehow more imposing, he stared back through eyes the colour of burnt Satsuma, from beneath a chestnut, out-of-control mane of hair. Questions and curiosity, as well as an underlying humour poured from his expression, and twisted the line of his lips.

A plum-sized blockage caught in my throat, one it took three attempts to swallow down, leaving my mouth as arid as kilned sand.

"How lovely to meet a local businesswoman," the man said, and I recognised the smooth tone instantly. "Especially one of the Harrington line."

"You took my calls." An obvious statement. "Which means you know of the arrangement, so there's no reason to stall with formalities."

His lips twisted further. On anyone else, they'd have looked like a grimace. On him, they seemed to hold an offering of delights. He nodded toward the sack I held. "You have the agreed amount?"

Agreed? He'd made the demand. I'd had no choice but to comply. "Twenty-five," I confirmed.

At a quiet command from the odd man, Ivan stepped forward and reached for the sack.

I tugged it back a little. "My friend first, if you'd be so kind."

The man's chuckle sounded like a bubbling geyser. "That's not quite how these transactions work."

"Maybe not in your head, but this is how they work when dealing with me. If you take your prize first and then renege in the exchange, I'm screwed. At least you have every hope of ensuring my end of the bargain is fulfilled with the backup you have here." I nodded toward his freaky aide, but as Goldie fast-sobered, I wondered what the hell I'd said wrong.

"You know what I am?" he asked, his tone as serious as death.

I'd no idea which of my words had given him that impression. Or maybe my face had done all the talking he'd obviously heard. Trying to school my features, I answered, *Honestly* … "No …" … *not for certain, anyway*.

"But you suspect."

Unable to come up with a truth *and* distraction fast enough to fool them, I refrained from answering that question.

"Mr Gold must think very highly of you to allow you so close."

I could have told him *Mr* Gold hadn't exactly had a whole lot of choice in the matter, but instead, I kept my mouth shut again—mostly because Ivan and his sucky interjection on what should have been a normal, pleasant evening was the only reason I'd ended up involved at all.

He patted Kellie's shoulder and waved her forward. "Okay, you may cross to your friend."

I could tell by her twitchy eyes and head, she didn't like showing the guy her back as she padded over the floor. She practically snatched at my arm the second she was close enough, her fingers digging into my flesh, even through my sweater and coat.

"Can we go now?" she squeaked through clenched teeth.

I nodded and held out the bag toward Ivan, though my gaze remained on the one who'd never even given his name. "I trust this is Benjamin's debt paid in full now?"

"It is." He smiled, once more adding intrigue to an already compelling face. "Though, you might want to call him off now …" So, he knew of Benjamin's presence. "… before he finds himself in a new batch of trouble."

"No worries," I muttered, backing Kellie and myself out of the room. Only at the archway did I turn us away.

"Ms Harrington?"

I glanced back to find those unusual eyes full of anticipation and a little closer, though I hadn't heard him move.

"I very much look forward to doing business with you in the future."

What the hell does that mean? screamed through my head as my pulse did a little stuttering act, but I ordered myself not to respond, not to allow him to see he'd unnerved me, and merely nudged Kellie in the direction of the front door.

We burst from the house and into the cold without interruption, and as soon as we had, I slammed the barrier in place, taking a moment on the top step to catch the breath I'd been holding. Fingers trembling, from way more than the temperatures, I wiggled Drake's mobile from my pocket and hit dial on the last received call.

After one ring, Drake's voice said, "Tell me that wasn't you I saw going into Rufus's house, Cole."

Rufus? I didn't quite contain my snort.

"Cole?"

"Yes, it was me. I have Kellie. You can call Benjamin off and tell him his dues are paid."

Silence met me. The stunned kind, I guessed.

I scoured the darkness, peering through the trees like I'd spot Drake peeking around one.

"I'll tell him," he said.

"Thanks." I started down the steps, Kellie's hold on my arm bringing her down with me. "You can also tell whoever owns the RAV4, thanks for the loan, but they'll have to wait on its return, because right now …" I sighed. "I'm going home."

Kellie shivered against me, as I hung up and pulled open the passenger door of the car. "What the hell happened tonight?" she asked.

I wondered how long it would take her. "It's a long story." I shrugged out of my coat and draped it around her shoulders. "One I'm not even sure *I* know."

"You are *so* sharing. And my being dragged off the sofa and hauled away by a couple of hulks had better have a decent explanation behind it."

Everything within me wanted to ask what had happened, how bad the evening had been for her, but something within the continued shivers of her body told me that moment wasn't the right time for the inquisition. "Tomorrow," I said, tucking into her seat. "I promise."

With a last glance toward the 'farmhouse', I rounded the car and settled behind the wheel. Air blew from the vents the instant I turned the key, and I aimed them all Kellie's way, before directing the car around the roundabout and onto the driveway.

"So … how was your date?" she asked.

I twisted toward her, caught the curve of her lips in the dark. "My date? It was … different."

I turned back in time to spot a golden bundle whizzing past the headlights.

My foot smashed down.

The tyres shifted to the left.

The car ground to a stop.

"What was *that*?" Kellie said.

Heart thudding loud enough to drown out all other sound, I stared at the empty spot, where I'd have sworn on my life I'd just seen something, too.

"It looked lik—"

A bang hit my window.

Kellie screamed, as I jumped a foot off my seat.

Benjamin's face peeked through the glass when I dared look that way. My door shot open. Hands gripped my shoulders. In the next second, I stood wedged against the vehicle with Benjamin's hands on each of my cheeks.

"Are you okay?" He scanned over my features. "Tell me he didn't hurt you. What the hell were you thinking, Cole?"

"I was thinking of getting my friend back and saving your hide."

"What did Rufus do to you?"

"Nothing. I paid him. He handed Kellie over. We left."

"That's it?" Disbelief tinged his tone.

I nodded.

He blew out a breath, seemed to relax a little. "I'm going to drive you home. I can do that much, at least." He stepped away—revealing himself in all his naked glory.

Again.

I gaped at him. "What happened to your clothes this time?"

He leaned in and popped the lever to the back hatch like I hadn't even asked.

I followed him when he headed for the rear of the car, trying hard not to get distracted by the sweet, sweet curve of his bum as it tick-tocked with each step. "I swear I've seen you without clothes more than with."

"And she says that like it's a bad thing," Kellie piped up from her seat.

I ignored her, dragging my gaze to Benjamin's eyes as he turned. "Are you going to tell me what's really been going on tonight?"

He opened the hatch, and pulled out a sweater, tugging it over his head.

"Maybe you'd like to start with what really happened in the park?"

He slid Jersey shorts over his hips.

I peeked inside the boot space, to find an entire holdall rammed with clothes. "How much does this kind of thing happen, exactly, Benjamin? I mean, you have a boot full of clothes. You run around with nothing on … and it's fricking *winter*, for God's sake. You all vanished without a trace earlier, only to have—"

Fingers clasped the back of my neck as lips smothered mine. I blinked, bringing his seriously close face into focus. For a moment, I lowered my lids and allowed the moment of what very much resembled calm to wash through me, only just succeeding in squashing the groan brewing in my chest.

When I opened my eyes, his seemed to glow in the darkness.

"You've already figured out the truth, and you refuse to believe yourself," he said quietly. "Come on. Let's get you home."

For a moment, I just stood there, trying to decipher his words, as he climbed into the driver's seat.

Or trying to accept them.

Getting nowhere fast, I yanked open the back door and lowered myself inside to Kellie's burning curiosity.

Her eyebrow arched up. "Different, huh?"

Grabbing my seatbelt, I gave a half-shake of my head. "Kellie, you have no idea."

5

Tucked beneath a duvet on the sofa, Kellie's snores made her sound like a hibernating bear. An early bird by nature, she'd pretty much crashed and burned after she'd gotten what she could out of me and Benjamin, which turned out to be not very much at all.

Listening to the gruff background tune, I stood on the front deck beneath the porch overhang and watched the sway of Benjamin's hips as he padded barefoot along my path. Despite my relief at the evening being over, I couldn't help the twinge of sadness as I watched each step carry him farther away.

Despite the ease with which Kellie had gone under, he'd avoided my questioning stares, batted my demands for answer. The fact that every time he looked at me, my insides went gooey, was neither here, nor there. Or how much my mind would rather be basking in the imprinted image of Benjamin's arse than dealing with the current situation.

Though, both of those just made his walking away a little harder to take, which probably made me the crazy person to ever walk the darned planet. Because I surely should've been rejoicing in it, thankful that the most eventful and frightening—and excitingly exhilarating—night of my life had come to an end and I could return to mundanity and obeying orders.

Reaching the end of the path, Benjamin halted, his hand on the gate. When he hadn't moved seconds later, my heart did an idiotic little thrum.

For what, though? Did I think he'd turn back around? Did I even want that?

I'd be insane to.

Right?

He spun and re-trod the path back toward me. I followed his every sure-footed move, until his climb of the bottom step below me brought him almost to eye level.

"Do you believe everyone we meet in life, we do so for a reason, Cole?" he asked.

My gaze flitted away and back to him. "Do you?"

He nodded, dipping his hands deep into his pockets. "Some people come into your life as blessings. Others as lessons."

My head tilted. "Which one are you to me, then?"

"Can't I be both?" he asked.

"Why, Benjamin?" My lips twitched. "What do you think you can teach me?" *Other than the world is a far freakier place than I ever imagined.*

"That wearing heels will likely get you killed."

"Moot lesson," I said. "I pretty much figured that much out myself, when a crazy, naked man caught up with me."

His chuckle arrived quiet as he climbed the second step. Closer, a little higher, his expression sobered as he faced me.

"And as for being a blessing? I'm ..." My breath hitched a little. "... going to take a little more convincing on that."

Hands still in his pockets, he ducked forward.

The closer he came, the more my eyes played irritating tricks on me, and that shock of honey blond of his seemed to suddenly surround more prominent cheekbones and a prouder forehead. His golden eyes, even half-obscured beneath lowered lashes, merged into those of the lion in the park.

I almost swallowed my tongue, but managed to untwist it just enough to blurt out, "Benjamin, are you a—"

He stilled. "What, Cole? What am I?"

"Are you a—I mean, did you ..." My brows pulled tight as his words hissed through my mind: *What am I, Cole?* I took a deep breath. "Can you turn into a lion?" I swallowed the second I'd asked the question, half dreading what trouble it'd just landed me in.

"Do you believe I can?" was all he said in response.

"That's a non-answer."

"It's an important question. Do you *believe* it?"

Nooooo, I wanted to screech. *I mean, how bloody ridiculous would that be?*

"Yes," I whispered.

I waited for him to affirm. He merely smiled, his gaze never wavering as he leaned in across the remaining inches and met my lips with his own.

A moan bubbled in the back of my throat at the connection. With no imminent danger, no surrounding woods, and no frisky creatures rolling about, I allowed myself to taste him, my moan escaping when a subtle muskiness drifted from his pores. Heat from his hands landed on my hips, before sliding around to my back, and beneath his demand, my body arched into him as his tongue swept along mine with delicious finesse.

Drawing back, he seemed to study me, and I couldn't help but notice how his eyes had darkened and resembled a couple of orange opals. I also couldn't help but notice how his hands lingered at my hips.

"Let me see you again, Cole." His whisper was a hoarse invitation that skated over my spine, and I very much wanted to throw myself at him and shout *yes!*.

Instead, I raised an eyebrow and drew back a little farther. "Are you kidding me? You're the most dangerous date I've ever had …"

"Probably the most exciting, too."

I shook my head, breathing out a scoffed laugh. "Not to mention that, at twenty-five grand a shot, you're the most *expensive* date I've ever had. *Thirty*, if you add in the agency fee."

"All the more reason." He shrugged, taking a step back as if it was required with 'business' on the table. "I could pay you back one evening at a time."

He had offered to repay the evening's added expenses during

the ride home. Multiple times. And I'd declined equally as often, but something about his offer then held my knockback on pause.

My eyebrows winged up. "You realise that'll take a seriously long time?"

He nodded, backing down the steps until his soles hit the path again, though he didn't quite contain the smile I could see teasing at his lips. "It just means I'll have to pick you up tomorrow at seven ..." Another backward step, the denim of his jeans hugging his movements. "And then I'll need to pick you up the next day at seven ..." A dip of his chin and an upward glance of his golden eyes from beneath his eyelashes accompanied his next step. "Then at seven the day after that ... and the day after that ... and then ..."

I let my gaze skim along his body, over his open shirt and tatty jeans, down to where his bare feet pressed into the snow, and all the way back up again to that handsome face and hair gone wild since the beginning of the evening. Somewhere between south and north, I felt myself melt as deeply as the snow beneath Benjamin's feet.

"Okay," I said, a smile creeping in. "You're on. It's a date."

ACKNOWLEDGMENTS

As usual, an author never works completely alone in order for a story to be fully born, so I'd like to thank …

Aimee Laine, for urging that I come up with a new story way back in 2011, which led to the craziness of this tale being formed;

The readers who took a chance on new authors six years ago, picked up a copy of the *Make Believe* anthology, and loved Ben and Cole enough for me to believe putting it back out there was the right thing to do;

My street team, for putting up with my sporadic absences this year and their continued patience. I love you, Book Babes;

Keri Lake, for always being supportive and honest;

And finally Mr B. Because whatever I'm doing, so long as I'm happy doing it, the guy never bats an eyelid. It's always only ever an enthusiastic 'Okay'.

And finally, finally to you. For grabbing this insane little story of mine. ♥

ABOUT J.A. BELFIELD

J.A. Belfield lives in Solihull, England, with the best husband in the world, aka Mr B, a couple of now-adult but cheeky as heck kids, a pooch she treats likes the baby of the house, and a cat that like to vomit in unnecessary places.
Although best known for her erotic romance THE THERAPIST, and the Holloway Pack series: THE WOLF WITHIN, BLUE MOON, CAGED, UNNATURAL, CORNERED, amongst other titles, she is currently trying her hand at about thirty different projects at once, in almost as many different genres.
Want to stay up to date on all things J.A. Belfield?
Want to discover what she's working on, as she's working on it?
Want to get sneak previews of her writing and covers and everything else upcoming?
Want to enter giveaways exclusive to her group?
To be in the know ahead of the crowd with J.A. Belfield's writing journey, join Book Babes today.
We'd love to have you!

Or visit: https://www.facebook.com/groups/BelfieldsBookBabes/

A HOLLOWAY PACK PREQUEL

BEGINNINGS

J.A. BELFIELD
INTERNATIONAL BESTSELLING AUTHOR

THE
A HOLLOWAY PACK NOVEL
WOLF WITHIN
J.A. BELFIELD
INTERNATIONAL BESTSELLING AUTHOR

A HOLLOWAY PACK NOVEL
BLUE MOON
J.A. BELFIELD
INTERNATIONAL BESTSELLING AUTHOR

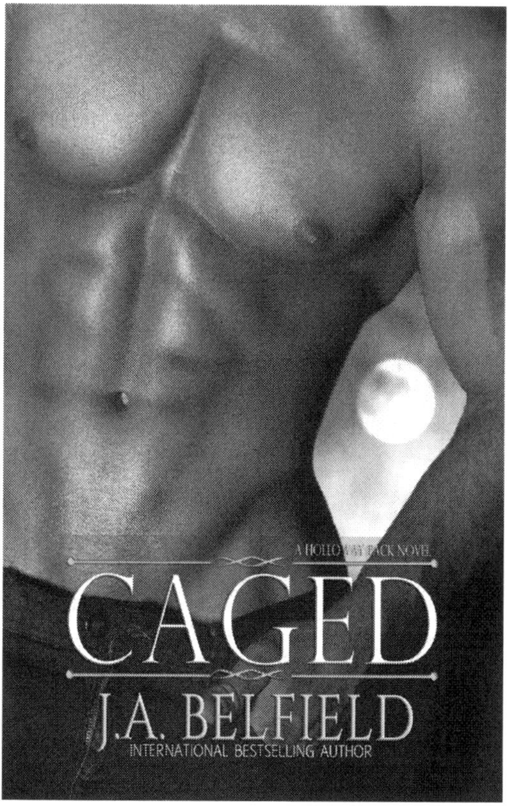
CAGED
J.A. BELFIELD
INTERNATIONAL BESTSELLING AUTHOR

HOLLOWAY PACK NOVEL
UNNATURAL
J.A. BELFIELD
INTERNATIONAL BESTSELLING AUTHOR

A HOLLOWAY PACK NOVEL
CORNERED
J.A. BELFIELD
INTERNATIONAL BESTSELLING AUTHOR

Chase Walker...
Sex Therapist
Extraordinaire at
your service

THE THERAPIST

INTERNATIONAL BESTSELLING AUTHOR
J.A. BELFIELD

Printed in Great Britain
by Amazon